A

BLACK AFRICAN

WIDOW

Precious Assah Sibitane. All rights reserved

A black African widow

A black African widow

Poetry collection

By: Precious Assah Sibitane

Precious Assah SibitaneAll rights reserved

A black African widow

Copyright © 2021 Precious Assah Sibitane

All rights reserved. No part of this publication may be reproduced, distributed or transmitted in any form or by any means, including photocopy, recording or other electronic methods, without the necessary written permission of the publisher. For permission request; write to the publisher at the address below.

ISBN: 9798701771428

Imprint: independently published

Write to:

Precious Assah Sibitane

Box 283, Sidlamafa 1332

Mpumalanga

South Africa

Email: assasibitane@gmail.com

Precious Assah SibitaneAll rights reserved

A black African widow

dedication

To

All poetry lovers

A black African widow

Precious Assah SibitaneAll rights reserved

A black African widow

CONTENTS

Contents

Precious Assah SibitaneAll rights reserved

A black African widow

Precious Assah SibitaneAll rights reserved

A black African widow

Precious Assah SibitaneAll rights reserved

PREFACE

A BLACK AFRICAN WIDOW

In this collection of poetry Assah is deeply concern about the way women and children are treated by the society especially when a man passes on. The inequality between man and women which perpetrate women and children abuse. She has looked at the history of all women and discovered that about 90% of women are suffering under the hands of abusive men. In the poem titled,' A black bleeding beauty,' she condemns the deeds of men and give hope to women and children liberation. She further urged all women to take a trip to themselves, find strength in themselves, depend in themselves and

A black African widow

learn to develop themselves to cab the issue of depending on men which gives rise to women and children abuse. She portraits a very loving space but full of disappointment when a woman asks his man to be her valentine which is in vain. She painted a picture on how great God is when she talkes about the beauty of nature in,' He is great.' She condemned Xynophobic acts in, 'The ugly monster,' saying in God's eyes we are one.

She portraits a picture on how neglected our police are, and how they are killed by the communities they are protecting on daily bases and condemns such a deed in,'I was born to die.' She left no stone unturned in,' The voice in the wilderness,' where she condemns the government on the treatment and value given to teachers. She condemns children abuse in, 'The bitter life of a black girl child,' and touched challenges like drug abuse and other life challenges,

Precious Assah SibitaneAll rights reserved

A black African widow

feed your soul and enrich your mind in the diverse collection of poetry, dance, cry, celebrate, pay tribute, pray and condemn.

Precious Assah SibitaneAll rights reserved

A black African widow

Chapter 1

1.   THE UGLY MONSTER

I might not be a South African,

But I am an African.

I might not be an African,

But I am a human being.

The Centre of it all is the blood,

I mean the same blood.

I might not speak your language,

You might not speak my language too,

I might have my own religion,

The Centre of it all understands.

Precious Assah SibitaneAll rights reserved

A black African widow

Home sweet home, the sweetest language

Enjoyed by families in their homes,

Who then can neglect his birth place for sweet?

Why some people are called amakwerekwere,

Why others are called amagrigamba

The Centre of it all is embracing and

Appreciating our differences.

Yesterday it was apartheid over blacks and whites,

Today it's black to black violence,

A black killing a black under the foolish umbrella of foreigners.

Precious Assah SibitaneAll rights reserved

A black African widow

The Centre of it all is humanity.

We may have our different agendas in life,

We have different opinions,

Different cultures and traditions,

Different colors and different languages,

But in God's eyes we are ONE

*Precious Assah Sibitane**All rights reserved*

2. SPEARS IN MY HEART

"Grow up my child you will see it"
"Grow old my child, you will see it,"
My granny used to say such words
My mother will always spit such sour words

When I ask them the meaning
Neither of them explained
They both sing in one chorus
It is a taboo to question elders.

Precious Assah SibitaneAll rights reserved

A black African widow

Yes I was grown when I experience
spears in my heart I lost a brother in two
illnesses

I couldn't understand, my heart was
stubbed everyday

In a week time I lost my father out of
stroke, yes spears in my heart.

When days are dark people will tell you
to try,

When things are bad, they will say pray

When everything is complicated, people
will say

When it is dark, dawn is approaching

Spears in my heart, I still can feel it

I have talked to people about it but,

Some laugh, some don't listen

Precious Assah SibitaneAll rights reserved

A black African widow

Some think I am crazy.

I feel better now as I am talking
Through my pen on this paper
Because it is listening but saying nothing.
I feel like the white color in this paper
Is saying, now it is ok
It feels like the black color is saying, it is
Enough with moaning let it go

Precious Assah SibitaneAll rights reserved

3.   A BLACK AFRICAN WIDOW

I cry, I lament, if my tears were
contained,

I would have filled a number of liters

I am still crying, I lament, and this is a
life time lament.

I am still standing at the back of my
house

Where my matrimonial bed is facing,

Looking at the heap of sand lined with
huge

Stones, the two yellow dishes has lost its

Colour, just on top, the basin I used to
wash

Your feet facing down looking at you.

Precious Assah SibitaneAll rights reserved

A black African widow

I cry, I lament, you made a promise to me,

For better or worse, through thick and thin,

But my king where are you now?

You said your people are my people,

But I am naked now, all we worked for

Is taken, I am left with your children,

Penniless and suffering.

Why did you have to go and leave us behind?

You lied to me.

You used to be honest to me, that was then,

When you said let's meet down the river,

Precious Assah SibitaneAll rights reserved

A black African widow

I would find you there waiting,
I would run to your arms for all the
hugs,
We use to meet at the market place,
You were always the first to wait,
Then I would join you with my basket
Which you would fill to the top
And help me carry it home.

These nights you keep calling me,
When I go out to that heap of sands,
You are not there, still the dishes and the
basin
I cry out loud, I…….lament………..

Precious Assah SibitaneAll rights reserved

A black African widow

When you visit my dream land, we chat together like before;

You make all the promises as usual

But when I wake up, you are gone.

Remember the other day when you were drifting

Away, I shouted, we miss you but you disappeared

I cry, I lament, I will lament till we meet again.

Precious Assah SibitaneAll rights reserved

A black African widow

4. AS I BOW

I pray to God that I don't fail you my baby

That as a mother I make you happy.

Guide and protect you.

I pray that you trust me as mom and trust God more I pray that you and I relate in a way that you feel all is well when we are together.

In my arms, you will always find warmth.

In my eyes love, in my mount, and words of wisdom.

I pray that I become more than a mom

So we share pleasures and downfalls.

Precious Assah SibitaneAll rights reserved

A black African widow

May the Man above make me………..
Strong enough to be your shield
Soft enough to pamper you with love
Patient enough to let you be, yet alert
enough to know when you are not well.

No matter how sensitive you may be,
May I welcome you and make you feel at
ease.
As we conquer life's ups and downs,
I pray that I love, protect and guide you
In the best possible way, that I'm the
best
Mom I can be.
So be it.

EUPHEMIAH CELUXOLO NTULI

Precious Assah SibitaneAll rights reserved

A black African widow

5.   A REASON TO BEAM

I was scared, I still am, but your appeal
didn't go unnoticed.

Even though I am confused about many
things noticed,

My love for you is promised.

Your little moments each day leaves me
promised.

You fill my heart with love

My soul with hope,

The two of us lives like a pair of dove.

All the sweet things makes me cope.

You feel my being with strength

Instill in me adoration.

Precious Assah SibitaneAll rights reserved

Which provides enormous motivation
Behold this will stretch some length.
You are my shoulder to lean on
May I be your chest to cry on?

EUPHEMIAH CELUXOLO NTULI

Precious Assah SibitaneAll rights reserved

Chapter 2

6.   I WAS BORN TO DIE.

I don't wake up because I don't sleep,

I don't sleep because I don't wake up.

Day and a night, all the same.

Even if I try to sleep, duty calls.

I was meant to die.

When I wear my uniform I feel content knowing

I am going to save my community,

To protect my people but I know it's over.

Precious Assah SibitaneAll rights reserved

A black African widow

When duty calls, I respond, like every worker,

I work…

With me it's different because I was born to die.

When others are in trouble, duty calls me,

Help that's what I offer, when thugs attack,

Duty calls me, which I respond smilingly

After work, only my mom appreciates.

When I arrest the wrongs, the community complains

When I don't arrest the wrongs, the community complains

Precious Assah SibitaneAll rights reserved

A black African widow

When others call for protection, I respond.

The very same caller kills me,

My sin is my duty and my duty calls.

I was trained to protect my killers,

Trained to love those who hate me most,

When I embrace this one,

The other one shoot me at the back.

I was born to die

All I ask, just when death strikes, tell my mom

She gave birth to a tomb

Tell my children I died for my people,

Precious Assah SibitaneAll rights reserved

A black African widow

The people who killed me.

Burn my body into ashes and let my kids save it.

Don't bury me; the earth might kill me,

I might die again because I was meant to die.

I don't deserve a funeral nor a professional Cop match,

I was born to die.

Precious Assah SibitaneAll rights reserved

7.   I AM A GENUINE AFRICAN

Look! I was born in a compound not in a house

My cry was more than loud, because I was born

In a hut not hospital.

My baby cry was irritating as I needed a name,

Not just a name but my ancestral name "Lomalanga."

Yes, I am a genuine African.

I was born through my biological mother,

Look! I had four mothers, all equally valued.

Precious Assah SibitaneAll rights reserved

A black African widow

I had a number of brothers and sisters,
All equally valued.
Of course I am a genuine African.
I was born out of polygamy
I am the product of bigamy

Look! I have learnt to share
I have learnt to eat in one dish
With my siblings
Really I am a genuine African.
I grew up sleeping on a mat; a blanket
was history Except for an animal skin.

Precious Assah SibitaneAll rights reserved

A black African widow

I owe it down to the valleys of Lebombo
Mountain,

Which glues up, South Africa,
Mozambique and Swaziland I am an
original African.

I owe it down the Nkomazi River,
umlumati

And mgwenya which together compete
with Mozambique.
Indeed I am an original African.

CLAUDIAH THANDIWE NTULI

Precious Assah SibitaneAll rights reserved

8. THE VOICE IN THE WILDERNESS.

Let your voice be heard, you have access to

The presidents of tomorrow, you have access

To the doctors of tomorrow, you have access

To the leaders of tomorrow, so speak out loud

Let your voice be heard.

You were meant to be noble and professional

But money swallowed your noble status

Precious Assah SibitaneAll rights reserved

A black African widow

And made dull your professional status,

But rise; there is still time for your voice
to be heard.

The sweetest past of apartheid was the
recognition,

Of your status, yet democracy
demoralized your spirit

And left you demolished.

Apartheid considered the fact that you
are,

The foundation for every profession,

But democracy crushed you and left you
crawling like crushers.

It will be very difficult for you to climb
the ladder

Precious Assah SibitaneAll rights reserved

A black African widow

And change the behaviors of the so called "bosses"

So just leave them, nature will take its course.

It will be difficult for you to open closed ears,

Of the so called learned leaders as their little education

Failed to open them, but rise, there are ears open

Every day, prepared to listen to you.

Shout out loud; let your voice be heard

Preachers have preached about justice,

Singers have sung about it, but little education

Precious Assah SibitaneAll rights reserved

A black African widow

Has closed the eyes and the ears of leaders,

Rise; there are leaders of tomorrow whose

Ears are open and their eyes can see.

The platform is always yours,

Workers in big companies will never

Be heard as they have nobody to tell, they have

Nobody to plant the seeds of love, peace and

Justice, you have access to the future generation.

Precious Assah SibitaneAll rights reserved

A black African widow

Scream out loud, its time you teach the
Future generations about the source of
Love to avoid separations and divorces,
Time to teach the source of peace to
Make it prevail in days to come.
Time to teach the source of justice to
Avoid unjustness.

Like 'a,e,i,o,u" climb the ladder
Teach about love, peace and justice to build
A loving, peaceful and just generation.

Precious Assah SibitaneAll rights reserved

A black African widow

Precious Assah SibitaneAll rights reserved

9.   GAIN IN PAIN

The ground is made fertile through frost
And so shall our lives.
Our lives are made fertile through
disappointments and so shall it be.
When passing through predicaments,
Learn to say it is well with my soul,
When days are dark,
Learn to pray.

Pick joy in every sadness
Pick happiness in every sorrow.
Our gain is in pain
The bitter the pain, the sweeter the gain.

Precious Assah SibitaneAll rights reserved

A black African widow

Troubles and tribulations are actions
Allocated for individual beings.
Time is allocated for them too,
Accept them as they come
And let them pass.

Precious Assah SibitaneAll rights reserved

A black African widow

10. ALONE, LONELY IN THE LONELY LAND.

A dream, no I am awake and alive,

A thought, no I am alone in this lonely land.

A land of building and demolishing,

A land of giving birth and killing,

A land of loving and hating,

A land of joy and sorrows.

Dreaming in a live dream land,

Driving a motionless vehicle

Diving in a deep dark mad

Drifting away from my love dreams,

Drowning in deep thoughts,….maybe….

Precious Assah SibitaneAll rights reserved

A black African widow

Down to reality.

Alone, I learn to know myself better

Alone I visit my inner person,

Alone, I recall mistakes and mend them,

Alone, I raise the dead and chat with them

Alone I sing and dance,……who knows..

Alone, lonely in the lonely land, he will come.

Precious Assah SibitaneAll rights reserved

Chapter 3

11.   GO 2017 GO

I thought I was old enough to have seen things

I thought I have experienced experiences enough for my age.

But I was lying; you had a lot in your package,

You taught me to sleep in an empty stomach.

You taught me to beg for survival.

I thought that was enough,

I was stunned to realize that the candles for valentines were set dead by my own tears.

Precious Assah SibitaneAll rights reserved

A black African widow

I was traumatized one night when I
realized through a window,

My man making love to a school kid.

I mean I was permanently destroyed

When I realized my man was staying
with a teenager, Young enough to be his
granddaughter.

2017, is this not enough?

What else do you have in your package?

Do not drag your feet, just go, please go.

You changed pastors into liars, who are
you,

You really belong to hell.

The wounds you have opened will never
be healed.

Precious Assah SibitaneAll rights reserved

A black African widow

Enough is enough; you have left me with no Confidence in myself,

I have lost my self-esteem, nevertheless, you have taught me never to trust again.

 You have prompted me where human race comes from,

 And from now on, I will try to love but not to trust.

I've learnt that there is a very thin line between tears of joy and tears for sadness.

2017, you are the only creature I don't want to meet again,

And so die and don't wake up even in the eternity I hate you, GO.

Precious Assah SibitaneAll rights reserved

12.   HE IS GREAT

Watching a movie on bed, with the blinds striped aside,

I happen to have access to my garden, my own paradise.

Looking at the beauty of nature, my own beauty as it Reflects on the mirror,

My trivial hidden fancy eyes, slight attentive ears,

All decorated with the ever smiling face,

I came to realize how great God is.

Precious Assah SibitaneAll rights reserved

A black African widow

The birds singing on the other side of
the window, I realized that I am not
doing enough to show Him How great
He is but the birds do.

Looking at the sun striking on the
yellowish curtain

The yellowish summer sun-rails striking

With their different colors,

The scent I inhale stolen through the
open window,

 I happen to realize that God is a God of
order and His timing is perfect

Who am I to deserve this, who am I to
be reckoned special in such mercy.

God I thank you endlessly, you are great.

Precious Assah SibitaneAll rights reserved

13. THE FIRM FOUNDATION OF PEACE

Out of a bitter hurt heart, it is labored.

From a deep depressed soul it exhales out.

Within tight closed jaws, it appears.

Around a pale polluted face, it surfaces.

Through blocked nose, it slips out.

It stretches dead deaf ears.

In teary eyes, it shines out............

A SMILE......

The firm foundation of peace.

Hard to lay but guaranteed once done.

Precious Assah SibitaneAll rights reserved

A black African widow

It hides all pains from within.
It keeps the body healthy.
If it is not found from within,
Then nowhere else.
Even in the midst of storms and
Temptations, find it, it's not far but
within.

Success and happiness is measured
through it.
It has higher tests of manhood than
Battle ever knew.
The more we sweat in peace, the less
We bleed in war.
Find it, it's just within,
Smile and have peace.

Precious Assah SibitaneAll rights reserved

14.   I LOVE THEM

They full-fill my life

Boost my spirit.

They make me feel worthy a living.

Boost my self-esteem.

In them I meet doctors,

Architects, engineers,

Presidents and kings,

But all down to my level,

I mean my level.

They appreciate me when

The world makes a mockery.

They listen attentively,

They greet me with respect

Precious Assah SibitaneAll rights reserved

A black African widow

Coming from the bottom of their heart.
I love them.
They're flexible enough to be bent
When they lose direction,
A gesture is enough to direct.
My vacations are always
Longer without them.

Their absentia makes me feel
Alone, an orphan and not loved.
I can't wait to see their
Beautiful faces in colorful
Uniform, watch their zeal to learn.
I love them.

Precious Assah SibitaneAll rights reserved

15.   I AM AN AFRICAN

I am an original African.

This is demonstrated on the way I dress,

I don't fasten buttons but I tie a rapper.

I bid my body with colorful bids and ear-
rings.

My waist carries a number of them,
indeed I am an African.

Bold and beautiful.

I am an African.

This experienced through the eleven
official languages

That I am using to express myself,

Precious Assah SibitaneAll rights reserved

A black African widow

Ngiyakhuluma, ngiyabulabula,
ndiyathetha, ek praat,

Ndobvuwa.

I am an African.

Bold as I am.

Look at the different cultures, I have
access to,

The Nguni culture as it was fed by my
mother.

The Tsonga culture stolen from my
granny,

The Swati culture from my father' kraal,

Oh! Noooo, I love the fact that,

I am an African.

A genuine African.

Precious Assah SibitaneAll rights reserved

A black African widow

I dance different dances,
Shibhelane, umtsimba, sibhaca,
When in Venda ndatchina…..
When in swaziland ngiyagidza
Indeed I am an original African.
Boldly I bow.

Precious Assah SibitaneAll rights reserved

Chapter 4

16.   THE EDGE

No honest way to define it,

The only people who knows it,

Are those who have gone over it.

The edge…

A point of no reasoning

A point of stupidity

A point of blindness

A point reached by idiots

A point of foolishness

An edge…

Precious Assah SibitaneAll rights reserved

A black African widow

The edge or reaching the ceiling?
A point full of hungry lions at the back,
A river at its banks in front,
Two big anacondas left and right.
What is this?
The edge…

A point of less reason to breath
When everything loses meaning
When prayer becomes mumbling
A point of uselessness
In the edge…

I've learnt I'm better than myself
I've learnt to measure the distance
I can walk, the miles I can run.

Precious Assah SibitaneAll rights reserved

A black African widow

I've realized I am stronger than myself.
I have realized I can fly higher than…
The edge.

Precious Assah SibitaneAll rights reserved

17.   I AM AFRICA

From the top of Mount Kilimanjaro

Down the banks of River Nile.

From the hills to the valleys, the glades.

The trees, the flowers, the seas

Define my beginning, describe my
ending,

I am Africa.

The home of legend, Tata Mandela,

Home of fighters and peacemakers.

I am Angola, Uganda, Malawi, Burundi,

Rwanda, Namibia, Zimbabwe, Morocco,

Mali, Senegal, Ivory coast, Ghana,
Nigeria.

I am Africa.

Precious Assah SibitaneAll rights reserved

A black African widow

The mother to all races, colors and genders

The solace to victims of wars, oppression, poverty

And human degradation.

I have my flaws, I bear much struggles

I accommodate, I feed, I nurse, and I care.

I am Africa.

I am the king of wisdom

The prince of peace

I am a NO to xenophobia

A yes to love and caring

I am a NO to human trafficking

Precious Assah SibitaneAll rights reserved

A black African widow

A yes to UBUNTU
I am a NO to discrimination
A yes to humanity.
I am Africa.
Different races, my son
Different cultures, my daughters,
Different colors, my bosom friend
Different languages, the spice to my taste
Diversity is me
I am Africa.

Precious Assah SibitaneAll rights reserved

18. FAST KILLER

As I sit and wonder-

Why it feels like thunder?

I had it all under control,

All I wanted was to roll

Now you are my addiction

How do I get over this complication?

Just yesterday, we were friends

I had you in my hands

Suddenly we are in a war,

A battle of course

Will I ever win?

Precious Assah SibitaneAll rights reserved

A black African widow

You gave me smiles at some point,
You got me up high on cloud nine,
You made me touch the skies
Now I go crazy with each line.
I laugh for nothing.
It is evident that:

In you there is no health
No youth and no peace,
I have just aged within minutes
My shoulders are hanging,
My legs are sticks,

My skin is pale.
My mind is doomed,
I think slowly,

Precious Assah SibitaneAll rights reserved

A black African widow

I always complain,

I feel so sick and closer to death.

My dear drug I thought you were my healer

Now I know you are my fast-kill.

Let us part ways,

This brings us to the end of our friendship.

Precious Assah SibitaneAll rights reserved

A black African widow

19.   YOUNG LOVE

It started like a lifelong marriage,

Like hope to a soul badly damaged.

I thought death will do us apart,

Yet neither one of us is buried,

The heart broke itself with all

The feelings it carried.

In both our minds we have a future,

In reality we are an emotional torture.

Maybe you don't need a man in in your
life,

After all you are your mother's daughter.

Sometimes I fear I will never love again

With these feelings that remains,

Precious Assah SibitaneAll rights reserved

A black African widow

Our memories have become a source of pain.

The tone of your voice when you said

You'd stay, when friends are no more

In the darkest days of existence.

I believed in you, I believed in us

And all I am left with is an issue of faith.

As time goes by I hope you will see

All the goodness you brought out in me

With you by my side, your hand on my thigh

There are a number of struggles I would've survived.

Precious Assah SibitaneAll rights reserved

A black African widow

You were my Cinderella, and I had your lost shoe

I bet you couldn't lean on a shoulder that needed a shoulder to lean on too.

WRIGHT BRIAN LINDELANI NGOMANE.

Precious Assah SibitaneAll rights reserved

20.   #DRUGS MUST FALL.

Damn stupidity

I will fight till the last drop of my blood

Grind it till my last teeth grind itself,

If I lose my hands, I will kick it,

When I lose my feet, I will bump on it,

It's a real war, not a wow.

Drugs must fall.

I was born a leader

I was born a champion

A dreamer a go-getter a winner

Look now, I am a poor follower, I am a
beggar, all I can dream of, Is a piece of
cigar after another.

Precious Assah SibitaneAll rights reserved

A black African widow

I become a winner when I have taken more than others, drawing my death closer

Dagga must fall.

Look at me; I have dropped out of school

I have left my house, I am a real hobo.

The cold of winter eats me up

The heat of summer strike my head

Like hummer.

I have lost humanity,

I have lost my future.

Cocaine must fall.

I want my body back,

I want my youth back.

Precious Assah SibitaneAll rights reserved

A black African widow

I can't be a grandpa of 16 years,

I swear, I want my intellect back.

I want my time back.

Drugs, you ow me,

It's a war not a wow,

Nyaope must fall.

Precious Assah SibitaneAll rights reserved

Chapter 5

21.   ONLY YOU KNOW WHATS IN STORE FOR ME.

Battles in physique

Battles in finances

Battles in fiancé

Battles in emotions

Battles in work place

Battles in church

Battles in family

Battles in the house.

Dear God odein

Now I cast all unto you

Precious Assah SibitaneAll rights reserved

A black African widow

You created me,

You knew me before I was formed

You paved a way for me,

You protected me from all

Now I cast all unto you,

I cast all the burdens unto you.

Lord, only you know what's in store for me.

I am emotionally drained

I am physically drained

I am financially drained

Lord, I am psychologically drained

I am socially drained

Precious Assah SibitaneAll rights reserved

A black African widow

I am spiritually drained.

Lord, faith is the only pillar right now

My promise keeper

You have never lied,

Lord, I believe.

Through faith, I'm alive,

Through faith, I survived all

Through faith, I walk that walk

Ready to hold your hands one day.

Precious Assah SibitaneAll rights reserved

A black African widow

22. THERE IS MORE TO LIFE THAN IN HARDSHIPS

Hardships are time limited

Have a short life span

They never last

They always fail.

They come rolling like a rock, roll

Over someone, but guess what?

They roll over to the next one.

So take it as it approaches,

Roll it forward.

They are temporal surprises.

Precious Assah SibitaneAll rights reserved

A black African widow

They attack poor people,
Middle class and wealthy people.
They come in different routes
They wear different colors
They speak different languages
They belong to different cultures
But they are all failures.

When they strike, one go crazy
One forgets yesterday's victories
And forget God's promise
I WILL NEVER LEAVE
NOR FORSAKE YOU.
Some go mad and lose direction

Precious Assah SibitaneAll rights reserved

A black African widow

They move away from their stand points.

Hardship's temporal power May damage the mind.

Its strongest temporal Tsunami

Can blow a head off.

Its sharp blunt teeth can make

Bleed but a temporal bleed.

They bring wrong assumptions

They draw a wrong mind-map

Tell all the lies

Team up for solidarity

But always fail.

Precious Assah SibitaneAll rights reserved

A black African widow

Hardships are nothing but
Emotional growth.
They are part of our daily lives
Welcome it, box it and throw it over,
Someone is waiting for it.
It's a ball that everyone kicks,
So don't keep it, let it go.
There is more to life than
Temporal hardships.

Precious Assah SibitaneAll rights reserved

23.   IT'S NOT A WOW BUT A WAR.

Watching my body used up for a damn cent

Watching my time wasted over lollipops

Watching my parents waiting in vein

Watching my physique worn out,

My emotions

My spirit demolished.

Watching my shame, shared with a sugar daddy.

Watching the war covered in a wow.

The love of money, the root of evil.

The love of fame, the root of pride.

Precious Assah SibitaneAll rights reserved

A black African widow

The love of status, the root of shame.
The love of wealthy, the root of
greediness.
Look at me now, my breasts pointing
At my legs as if they are cursing them.
I am now older than my age.

This is a war not a wow.
My friends call it a wow
My friends enjoyed my company
For the sinful cent I earned to
Ruin my life.

My family clapped hands when
I brought home plastic bags
In exchange for my life.

Precious Assah SibitaneAll rights reserved

A black African widow

My relatives' rubbed my shoulders
In order to collect the
Left bread on my table.
I thought it was a wow, but it's a war.
As I am licking my wounds,
As I am taking this medication,
As I am dying,
My last words, 'there is no
Short-cut in life.
My voice of wisdom,
'Education is a key to success.
Selling bodies is a key to coffin.
This is a war to be fought
Not a wow to be celebrated.

Precious Assah SibitaneAll rights reserved

24.   WAY TOO SOON, BUT REAL.

Well build physically
Well measured height
Well scaled weight
Well shaped figure.

Oh my eyes say it again,
This is beyond my experience
I am damn traumatized
This is unbelievable.

You came via a private call
Which I ignored, not knowing
What is hidden in the round
Headed letter 'P'

Precious Assah SibitaneAll rights reserved

A black African widow

Nature intervened,
 I picked, the strange call with a stranger
But sweet confident male voice,
I sensed where the voice came from.
I was eager to face the challenge
I called out of fear when I reached

That restaurant, trying to trace him
He picked and romantically
Said, 'my hand is up.'
There he was, we greeted but…..

I was totally lost in paradise
It was not a debate but a speech
Contest, I was already fluttered.
He asked if he can steal my heart,

Precious Assah SibitaneAll rights reserved

A black African widow

I said, 'don't even steal it
But take it.
That was it,
Way too soon but real.

Precious Assah Sibitane ***All rights reserved***

25. HYPOCRITES

Call them aspirants

I call them deceivers

Call them dissemblers

I call them impostors

But they are heartless hypocrites.

They feed themselves at the expenses others

People's blood, parasites

They fish outside water but

Catch fishes.

Precious Assah SibitaneAll rights reserved

A black African widow

They hunt inside houses and
Catch wild animals, scavengers.
Identify them:
Their tongues utters no love
But property they don't even own
They drive big luxurious cars they don't
even own.

Be extra careful:
They wear themselves in sheep's clothing
Disguising in an Innocent child's
underwear.
Their conceal their wickedness with a
smile to launch an attack.

Precious Assah SibitaneAll rights reserved

A black African widow

They eat from plates of widows

They steal from orphans

They open the mouths of single mothers
and forcefully take

What's already chewed and eat.

They steal from their own parents.

They are heartless

Their blood must be cold

They are senseless

Their veins must be doubled

They are selfish

Their mouth spit blood

They have doomed people's lives.

Dear God, say something

You said sins are equal

Precious Assah SibitaneAll rights reserved

A black African widow

Please revise this and cry out loud

Can hypocrites be forgiven?

When you come back?

Are we going to share Paradise With them.?

God forbid.

They are worse than physical

Killers because they draw people

Closer to our God.

Hypocrites hurt and kill emotionally.

They cause pain so severe.

They leave victims with wounds

That will never stop bleeding.

God, please forgive them

They don't know what they are doing.

Precious Assah SibitaneAll rights reserved

Chapter 6

26.   A BLACK BLEEDING BEAUTY

Her eyes access some miles afar,

Ears as vigilant as a hunting cheetah

Her nose captures even a smell of clean water

Her mouth shouts as loud as a hungry lion.

Her forehead has big bleeding wounds

Wounds that never heal

Her heart is pierced into pieces,

Never has she tasted peace.

Precious Assah SibitaneAll rights reserved

A black African widow

Her little happiness is always disturbed
by another cut on the same bleeding
wounds.

Her tears never dry out, one tear is
deleted,

By the other to give way to another up
Until her beautiful chins become a water

Channel that waters the cruel earth.
Her heart oozes blood in a double way,
Her mind has become a dry desert,
Where no green shall ever grow,

A black bleeding woman.
Her tongue has never tasted love
Except for lust and lies.
Her body has never been cuddled

Precious Assah SibitaneAll rights reserved

A black African widow

Except for the benefit of sexual crisis
A black bleeding woman.
Her throat carries a poisonous fluid
As that of a serpent.
Her tongue spits acidic saliva,
She's a black bleeding woman.

She is politically oppressed,
Gender oppressed and discriminated,
She is brutally beaten and serially killed.
Even in church, she is dictated on how
To dress up and how to conduct herself.

She has names from same perpetrators:
She is called a widow if she loses her
man,
She is a prostitute if she does not have a
man,

Precious Assah Sibitane All rights reserved

A black African widow

A barren woman if she does not have a
child

But above all she is indeed a black
bleeding woman.

She has lost herself,

She has lost her self-esteem,

She has been judged until she judged
herself

Of course she is black and bleeding.

Check out ……

Woman of integrity

Woman of substance

Stand up, cover your wounds,

Stop that bleeding.

There is light at the end of the tunnel

Wipe those tears, clear your vision,

Precious Assah Sibitane   All rights reserved

A black African widow

Down there! The grass you've been
Watering has grown,
Dawn is approaching.
Your freedom is hidden under your left
Breast,
Your success under your beautiful hair.
Your life is never tied to somebody else's

Invest in your own self development.
Care more about what God says you are,
Enjoy your freedom…

Precious Assah SibitaneAll rights reserved

A black African widow

27.   A TRIP TO MYSELF

I travelled a short distance to my primary
school, a distance to my high school.

I travelled almost all provinces,

All countries,

I travelled the world.

I met different people, some influenced

My life for better, some for worse.

I've learnt different cultures.

Different languages.

I played their sport, sang their songs,

In fact I compromised myself for them.

I tried to understand their religion,

I danced for their rhythm.

Precious Assah SibitaneAll rights reserved

A black African widow

I loved them, sacrificed my life for them.

Let me take a journey now to my heart,

A trip to my inner self.

Let me be aware of myself

I am embarking on a project about
myself.

I have rated myself through others,

Let me rate myself by myself.

I have lived my life on survival and

Object referral mode,

I have defined myself through

People and possession.

Let me define myself through myself.

As I reached my inner destiny,

I have embarked on an investment,

Precious Assah SibitaneAll rights reserved

A black African widow

I want to invest in my personal development

That's the best gift I will ever give to myself.

28. DEATH YOU SHALL DIE

You! Cruel thief!

You! Foolish coward!

Listen, how foolish you are:

We use you as a donkey to carry us home,

You are a heartless machine

To drive us across the ocean to our home,

The home we always long for.

You are our damn ship to sail confidently

Precious Assah SibitaneAll rights reserved

A black African widow

To our Father.

You are a jealousy thief who remains searching.

You search and kill.

We die and dive to eternity, where

You will never qualify to be, not even

Your stinking venomous tail shall qualify.

So what, a shame on you!

Your day shall come, when you are going

To account for each of us.

I can't wait to see you taken, shuttered

Buttered and doomed for eternity.

DEATH YOU SHALL DIE.

Precious Assah SibitaneAll rights reserved

29. SINGLE MOMS OF AFRICA

LOOK AT THE SCENERIO

Imagine a body without a head
Imagine a firm without a head
Imagine a school without a principal
Imagine a country without a president
So is a home without a father.

Look at the scenario
When other children wake – up and run to
Their fathers to say good morning while a child
From single mom has covered his face with

Precious Assah SibitaneAll rights reserved

A black African widow

Shyness to say good morning to a crying mom.

When fathers are providing a single mom will say

Baby everything will be fine,

When fathers are taking their children to school,

A child from a single mom will walk barefooted

On the side of the road to school.

When fathers are taking their children for holidays

A child from a single mom will be making shapes

With mud and wires.

When fathers are playing with their children at home

Precious Assah SibitaneAll rights reserved

A black African widow

A child from a single mom will be asking questions like

'Mom who is my father'

Dear God when shall it be, come and change the situation

If being a single mom is caused by divorces, I was going

To urge the government not to grant divorces,

If being a single mom is caused by death I was going to ask God to intervene

Our mothers' faces have turned into big rivers of tears,

Their eyes are red like fire, their lips are wrinkled

Precious Assah SibitaneAll rights reserved

A black African widow

Their chins look like they have never tested oil.

Their expressions are bitter.

Brothers and sisters, lets plan our futures under the firm Pillars of good choices, lets us not be perpetrators towards single mothers

Mothers, it is said that your hearts are deep oceans

Of secret, but it is time you voice out what you feel

And stop saying everything will be fine

Precious Assah SibitaneAll rights reserved

A black African widow

30. Be my valentine

The thoughts of it which the mind
cannot deny.

How many valentines I should have
spent sweetly

If disappointment was absent,

Please this time be my valentine.

Because of your disappointments, I am

Disillusioned in real life,

I am disappointed in me

I am disappointed in true lies

I hate myself for everything

The face of disappointment strikes

Straight through my heart, it takes away

Precious Assah SibitaneAll rights reserved

A black African widow

My energy and tears my hope apart.

Nope, I don't want it this time.

The value of my soul falls below zero and

Becomes unreachable by any given hero.

The amount of effort I give is pointless,

When I seek help from friends, they laugh

And say,

"Dump him, he doesn't love u"

How I wish I could but my eyes cannot look at another man's eyes, let alone the rest.

I am bleeding inside, suicide all around, am i

The next victim? Nooooo? Mom said its selfishness.

Precious Assah SibitaneAll rights reserved

A black African widow

Cannot disappoint her, let me try.

I am on my Own now, I must be strong, let me try.

During my last valentine, as the day dripped by slowly Like molasses from my fingertips, I heard nothing, Not a smile, a sigh, not a look from your eyes and

Not a sideways grin, I didn't touch your soft lips, yes I didn't.

I can't seem to get the hurting to stop, emotions run deep

And I can't let it drop. You once breezed into my life,

Embraced me, but now I am left with this churning and deep

Sense of loss, you are smiling as if there is no cost at all.

Precious Assah SibitaneAll rights reserved

Chapter 7

31. My life, my story

From the time when I was conceived

The time when I was brought to life

I knew that life had begun.

I thought life was chocolate and lollipops

I thought life was to cherish and love the world

I didn't know about tears and sorrows,

All I knew was my mom's breast and my breath.

I knew only of the beautiful sky,

The smell of the dust of the soil,

Precious Assah SibitaneAll rights reserved

A black African widow

The beautiful music of birds,
The touch of dirty mud
The taste of the delicious honey milk,
That was my mother's breast,
The sound of African music and
The look of traditional dances.
Trouble began; trouble was in the house,
The devastating divorce of my parents.

The longing of my father's love,
Insecurities and shattered dreams,
Living with fear of losing my mom,
Wishing I was never born.
The bad choices my parents took,
The traumatic experience.
The sickness, witchcraft I heard about,

Precious Assah SibitaneAll rights reserved

A black African widow

The hatred and presence of my neighbors,

Neglected and gossips I heard and saw,

The story of my life was unbearable.

Sleeping in an empty stomach,

Going to school without lunchbox,

Going to school barefooted in winter colds,

Watching my mom's tears day and night,

Experience unbearable

Precious Assah SibitaneAll rights reserved

32. Justice

(My sonnet)
The ever mentioned, ever needed,
Yet remained unpracticed.
With state it is unquestioned,
Justice the most wanted.
Life has become a lie,
The innocent become guilty
The sweet has become salty
Yet justice remains a lie
Men and woman are silenced
Some are distanced
People are killed emotionally
Some are killed physically
But still justice remains unborn
When shall justice be born?

*Precious Assah Sibitane**All rights reserved*

A black African widow

33. I was deprived of my god – given self

If any amount of tears would stop this,

I was going to fill – up an ocean amount,

The kneel down and pay in exchange

For my God – given self.

When I asked for bread, I was given a stone,

When I asked for fish, a snake,

My life, a hell – whole.

When I reported I was crushed into pieces,

To shut up my big mouth,

If that be heard, what are we going to eat?

Where are we going to stay?

Precious Assah SibitaneAll rights reserved

A black African widow

I called him a father, "he called me his child,"

But he didn't respect that.

I trusted him but he was killing me cruelty

I had no choice but to watch my self-ruined.

I remained silent, kept wondering

If that was my destiny.

Each day with my mom's absence was hell,

My heart grew into a hard stone.

I lost my identify

I lost my dignity

I lost my stage

I lost my God – given self.

Precious Assah SibitaneAll rights reserved

A black African widow

34.   My enemies, my penicillin, I thank you.

There is no win without a fight.

There is no thrill in easy sailing when

There skies are clear and blue.

There no victory without temptations.

The conquering of Jericho was

Through the crossing of Jordan.

Tough times never last

Though people do.

Tough drivers drive on crocket dusty roads

Tough dogs never chase a parking car

Tough drivers do not park and chase

The barking dogs,

Tough drivers add more speed and move.

Precious Assah SibitaneAll rights reserved

A black African widow

So my enemies you are a useful drug that
Keeps me going.

So my friends fear not, for you have won
The battle.

Like an iron bent but do not break,

Like firm pillars standstill,

For its time to endure mighty
satisfaction.

For its time to pass from the world of
hopefulness

So your enemies are the drugs that heal
the

Dreaded disease called fear,

They sharpen you into a sharp spear,

They scrub the scales in you and leave

You smooth like a fish to be cooked.

My enemies, my penicillin, I love you

Precious Assah SibitaneAll rights reserved

35. Dedicated to my mother ladlamini.

For all the million things you gave to me,

For all the tears you shed to save me,

The bitterness you endured to raise me,

The sacrifices you undergo to protect me.

Indeed you are a woman of substance,

You are never shaken by any circumstances,

You maintained and sustained the family name,

My mother LaDlamini, you are wonderful.

You have been there for us through thick n thin.

Precious Assah SibitaneAll rights reserved

A black African widow

In the poverty stricken community,

In the poverty stricken family,

Mom you shined like the morning star,

You put food on the table,

You covered our nakedness.

It was your priority to see the family happy,

If there was a problem, I would read it from your eyes,

You always cried to make us laugh.

Gentle yet so strong, super mom,

You are a dependable source of comfort,

A teacher, a nurse and a counsellor.

I can't comprehend how you became a cook,

A doctor, a teacher and yet a play mate.

Mom when I look at you I see a walking miracle,

Precious Assah Sibitane ***All rights reserved***

A black African widow

Your unfailing love without limits,

Your ability to sooth all my hurts

Mom without you, there would be no
me,

You guidance have made me who I am,

Without your direction and purpose,

I would be lost and wondering aimlessly.

The joy, contentment and peace I have

Relates to you and your loving care
mom.

LaDlamini, you are the angel who
brought me

Into being and watched over me.

Mother you are wonderful.

Precious Assah SibitaneAll rights reserved

Chapter 8

36.   THE BITTER LIFE OF A BLACK GIRL CHILD.

I was born to pay the debts of my parents,

Yet I don't blame them, I blame the situation they found themselves in.

I was meant to carry the whole load of my siblings

Yes I was created to be exiled for the sake of my family.

Like every young girl I grew up with dreams,

I grew up with wishes,

I had my role models, but I was not meant to wish,

Precious Assah SibitaneAll rights reserved

A black African widow

I was meant to carry heavy burdens.

I was born to endure the pain of what my family

Enjoy today, yes I was meant to carry my proof family

Like every child I was thinking that one day,

I am going to progress my family, yet I was late.

The words I can still hear are, 'this is the man you Are going to stay with."

I couldn't ask how, why and when.

Within a twinkle of an eye a woman was made out Of me,

This is when my bitter life started.

I bitterly bare children out of pains, I was made

A legal slave, I wish I could have served my

Precious Assah SibitaneAll rights reserved

A black African widow

Life sentence in prison than in the place where

Everyone thought I was safe and happy.

When I was serving that sentence, friends, relatives

And even children of God new I was suffering

But no one offered help.

Time came when I decided enough was enough

When I wanted my voice to be heard, Pastor started

Preaching the gospel of, "through thick and thin"

I couldn't listen to them, my dreams were calling

Precious Assah SibitaneAll rights reserved

I wanted to go back to school to set a wakeup call

To the next generation about my slavery.

My life was made bitter as I was a child, yet it

Remained my choice to make it sweeter.

Like I endured the sweet pains of my bitter Life, I enjoy my freedom. When I free my self

Community leaders said I was disrespectful

Yet I was respecting my feelings, yes I free myself.

Precious Assah SibitaneAll rights reserved

37.   A TRIBUTE TO MY BROTHER ELLIOT

Not a single day goes by without your picture planted in my heart.

Not a single minute goes by without your laughter smeared in mind.

Not a single second goes by without your voice being heard.

That was late Monday last week.

The skies grow darker and dull, demanding your sweet soul,

The cloud clamored and cleared for a while as they were

Sad to witness such an unacceptable death.

Precious Assah SibitaneAll rights reserved

A black African widow

 The sun went so shy that it hidden itself deep into the stomach of the sky.

We all cried loudly, it was for the first time I heard such a cry

We scream loudly saying the ark of the family is taken.

It is taken for a life time captivity, the ship has sunk. The pool

Of luminaries has gone dry to expose vulnerable species.

The back born of the family is broken, the pillar of strength

Is gone, not just gone but forever.

A true family heart went weaker and weaker till it fell,

The once blossoming heart blacked and blocked down.

You are gone, not just gone but

Precious Assah SibitaneAll rights reserved

A black African widow

FOREVER

REST IN PERFECT PEACE.

38.   WALKING AWAY FROM A FAILED UNION

Left broken, vulnerable and lacking self-worth.

IIurting myself by hating myself.

I've learnt that healing hurts more

Than the wound self.

Letting go requires understanding

Self-worth and self-truth.

Requires accepting that I contributed

To my own miseries, by believing things will be ok.

Precious Assah SibitaneAll rights reserved

A black African widow

I ignored every red flag not because of love

But I was afraid to be alone.

I woke up on a heavy heart and slept

On a heavier heart.

Sadness and anger, the two feelings

I could relate to.

I loved hearing sad news so I cry out loud,

I related to violence so that I can release my anger.

Dear God, help me love and value myself,

Dear God, help me identify the things

I don't want to settle for.

Precious Assah SibitaneAll rights reserved

A black African widow

Dear God, help me protect my peace
And differentiate which battle to fight
for
And which to let go.
Dear God, help me to be kind to myself
And trust my instincts and intuition.
At least I am GRACEFULLY broken
As I am learning so much about myself.

Precious Assah SibitaneAll rights reserved

A black African widow

39. A TEACHER'S PRAYER

When I'm laid to rest:

Close my eyes because I want to look cute.

But my inner eyes will never be closed until

A South African child is liberated from poverty.

Close my ears,

But they will always be open to listen to a learner's cry.

But please DO NOT close my mouth,

I want to speak, I want to sing,

Till a South African child is liberated
From speech barrier.

Precious Assah SibitaneAll rights reserved

A black African widow

I want to shout till I am heard.

When I lay to rest, DO NOT put a cover on my head,

I want to think,

I will not relax my mind till all Female figures are liberated, liberated from gender inequality.

I want think till I psychologically understand the mind of a poor South African woman.

When I lay to rest, DO NOT close my coffin,

I don't want to miss the ever changing curricula

Precious Assah SibitaneAll rights reserved

A black African widow

Accompanied by ATPs, decorated by my own hand written lesson plans. When I lay to rest , GIVE me a piece of chalk, which will be a true reflection

That on earth I worked for DUST, in DUST ,I am DUST and I am going back TO DUST.

Precious Assah SibitaneAll rights reserved

40.   AS THE CLOCK TICKS…...

I lied to myself, listening and accepting your lies.

I hate myself for believing in you and the relationship we had.

Things went so fast, made me commit fast.

I didn't know within a clock tick I will be vulnerable.

I called as usual, you ignored my calls.

I tried harder, but all in vain.

The pains got higher and higher as labor pains.

I would cry from morning till morning,

But wearing a smile to bribe my children.

Precious Assah SibitaneAll rights reserved

A black African widow

I called you for days, you picked and warned me

Not to call, you are driving.

I could sense someone was in the car with you.

The pains got higher, I was afraid of my feelings

I tried….you pushed me away.

Let me tell you this tale, when you pushed me away,

The pains were higher and I was losing a

Dozen percentage of love.

When trying harder I was also losing harder,

Until all was gone.

I would watch you on line but when I text,

You didn't text back.

Precious Assah SibitaneAll rights reserved

A black African widow

I wanted to come to you

But you denied me access.

Let me tell you this tale, I wasn't
desperate,

But I was protecting the gold we dug
together.

Protecting the plans we planned
together.

I was respecting the vows we vowed
together.

You pushed me away.

I felt so alone and lonely,

I was so sick inside,

Dying each day and every day,

Holding my phone where ever I go,

Thinking you would call.

Precious Assah SibitaneAll rights reserved

A black African widow

As the clock ticks, I cried and lose.

Until I was left with nothing for you.

As the clock ticks I became a free woman,

I am free from your bondages of fake love.

Time is the best teacher it teaches better endings,

Time is the best teacher; it teaches the heart not a book.

Time is the best healer, it heals bleeding wound.

Time …tick!…tick!…tick!

I am a woman again.

Precious Assah SibitaneAll rights reserved

Chapter 9

41.   MY SON

My son, My blood

No single day goes by without you visiting

My mind, my peace, my thoughts.

My agony, my bitterness and my pains are

The places you always travel in my world.

You know what:

When you step down your feet, begin to walk,

I feel pains strong as if someone is pushing

Precious Assah SibitaneAll rights reserved

A black African widow

A sharp needle in my heart.

When you move around my agony,

I hide my face but my inner eyes begin to weep.

When you dive in my bitterness,

The pains are stronger than those I felt When I gave your birth.

That other night I begged you not to visit,

You are digging the bleeding wound,

But I was the one waiting for you.

Your painful tours brightens my world

Your visits may be painful but they remind Me of my status, I AM A WOMAN.

Precious Assah SibitaneAll rights reserved

A black African widow

Mary of the bible laid the foundation
When she lost her son Jesus Christ.
Who am I to deny endurance every
Women go through.
The pains of loving you my son,
The miseries I go through,
The pains of being a mother,
All I endure day and night,
And shall I endure for the rest of my life.

Let me hide my bitterness to the fact
that,
Your grave makes me a strong woman.
Your dusty coffin reminds me I was
once
On labor, where I earned my first
victory.

Precious Assah SibitaneAll rights reserved

A black African widow

The flowers and messages on top of

Your grave, marks my Last victory

My goodbye

My farewell

You're ever smiling face, always wipe

My tears and brightens my day and give
new hope.

May your seed grow and give rise to
lives.

You will ever be missed.

Precious Assah SibitaneAll rights reserved

A black African widow

ABOUT THE AUTHOR

➤ Precious Assah Sibitane is a vibrant humble high school teacher, a poet and a writer. A hard working teacher who conducts Debates, speech contests and poetry recitation. A grade 12 teacher who prepares learners for drama and poet from grade 8, a teacher who committed herself into preparing learners for public speaking.

➤ Born and raised in one of Mpumalanga's very remote and poverty stricken Trust called Mgobodzi.

➤ Raised in an area where, because of poverty some parents prefer exchanging their daughters with old men in order to

Precious Assah SibitaneAll rights reserved

get money for survival, where girls do not go to school because they are undermined as strangers who will leave the family when getting married.

➤ She was raised by her father, a pastor and a well- disciplined women who, despite all the above challenges she managed to work in the fields and pay school fees for her children and produced the author who is a qualified teacher.

➤ A place where women , especially widows would be deprived of their husband's properties when their husbands have passed on.

➤ Looking at all the above the author of this book developed a concern about women and children abuse, hence the Title,' A BLACK AFRICAN WIDOW.'

➤ A woman who enjoyed life when her husband was still alive and when the husband passed on, the in- laws took

Precious Assah SibitaneAll rights reserved

A black African widow

everything that belongs to her.

➢ As a widow she feels betrayed by the husband who promised to be the through thick and thin but now he is gone and brought all the sorrows endured by the widow and the children.

➢ The collection is mostly about women and their agonies in life which are brought by- by men, a touch on love and its consequences and a touch on drugs and other life challenges.

Precious Assah SibitaneAll rights reserved

www.ingramcontent.com/pod-product-compliance
Lightning Source LLC
Chambersburg PA
CBHW071330140726
47996CB00005B/1900